TRANSFORMERS
REVENGE OF THE FALLEN

HarperCollins®, ®, and HarperEntertainment™
are trademarks of HarperCollins Publishers.

Transformers: Revenge of The Fallen: Operation Autobot
HASBRO and its logo, TRANSFORMERS, the logo and all related characters
are trademarks of Hasbro and are used with permission.
Printed in the United States of America.

For information address HarperCollins Children's Books,
a division of HarperCollins Publishers, 10 East 53rd Street, New York, NY 10022.
www.harpercollinschildrens.com

Library of Congress catalog card number: 2008940053
ISBN 978-0-06-172966-9
Book design by John Sazaklis
09 10 11 12 13 UG 10 9 8 7 6 5 4 3 2 1
❖
First Edition

OPERATION AUTOBOT

Adapted by Susan Korman

Illustrated by MADA Design, Inc.

Based on the Screenplay by

Ehren Kruger & Alex Kurtzman & Roberto Orci

HARPERENTERTAINMENT

An Imprint of HarperCollins*Publishers*

Screech! Military vehicles squealed to a stop. A team of soldiers roped off an area for a top secret operation. They were tracking down dangerous aliens named Decepticons!

Soldiers leaped from the back of a pickup truck. The truck switched into the powerful Autobot Ironhide! Suddenly, the Tracker blipped furiously. The enemies were close!

"Sideswipe, deploy!" commanded Ironhide.
A semitruck opened and Sideswipe, a silver Corvette, shot out. Sideswipe changed into a robot armed with swords.

The Twins arrived to help. "You just try to stay out of trouble, okay?" Ironhide told the mischievous robots.

The team tracked the signal to a construction vehicle parked near some cement pipes.

Bam! The pipes were hurled aside as the machine changed into a giant Decepticon. It was Demolisher!

Another Decepticon, in the form of a European sports car, peeled out from behind Demolisher. The two villains raced down the street. "Track them!" shouted Major Lennox. "Don't let them get away!"

The sports car ripped through narrow alleyways. The Twins tried to follow, but the space was too tight!

The Decepticon switched into his robot form, bursting through a brick wall!

The Autobots fired missiles at the enemy that shredded the sports car's steel skin, but the wounded 'bot got back up.

Suddenly, Sideswipe roared up to the scene. He used his swords to slash at the 'bot.

The Decepticon fought back, sending a powerful energy pulse across the ground. The blast rippled down the street, rushing toward Sideswipe!

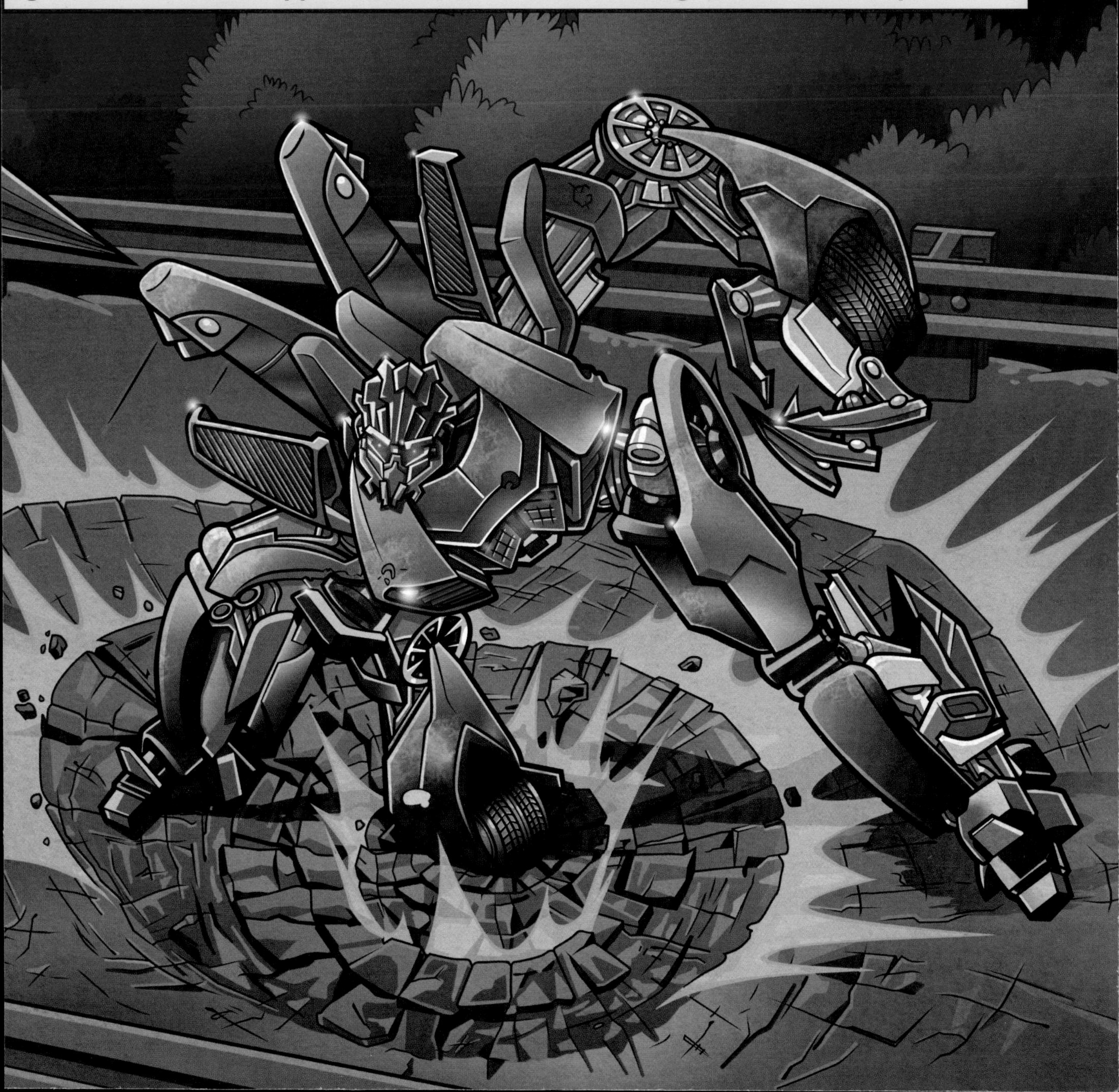

Sideswipe sprang out of the way just in time and advanced toward the Decepticon. With one swift motion, Sideswipe flipped the Decepticon's legs into the air, stopping it for good.

But Demolisher was still on the loose!
"Air support!" Major Lennox commanded.

A huge plane flew low over the city. The cargo hold opened to drop a semitruck. It was Optimus Prime—the commander of the Autobots!

Optimus sped after the massive Decepticon. Demolisher stood on one wheel, flipping end-over-end. As he rolled along, he crushed cars and everything else in his path!

Optimus switched into robot mode, jumping onto Demolisher's back!

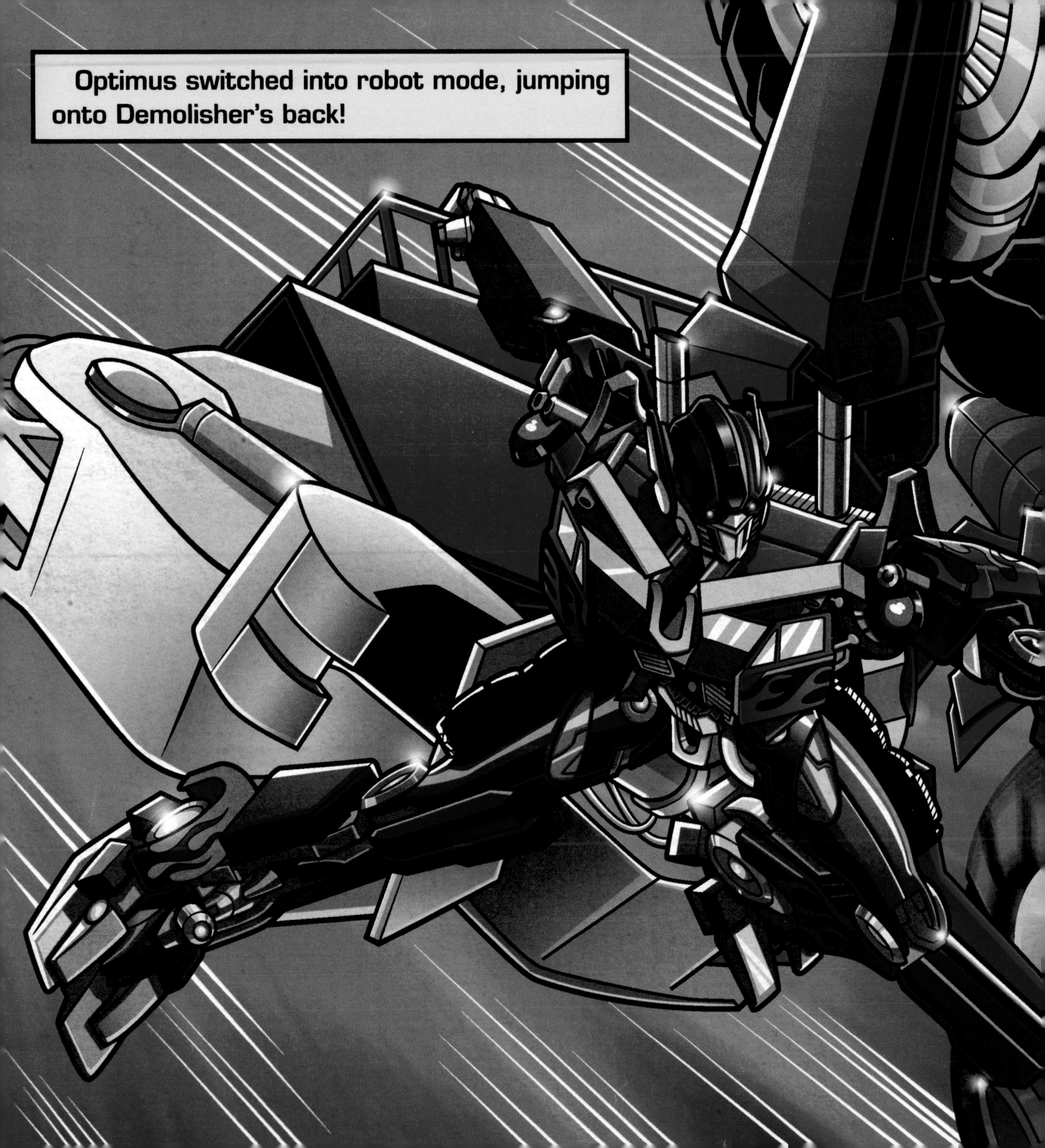

Meanwhile, Ironhide slid under Demolisher's giant frame and then swung onto one of his wheels. Together he and Optimus slammed into the Decepticon from both sides.

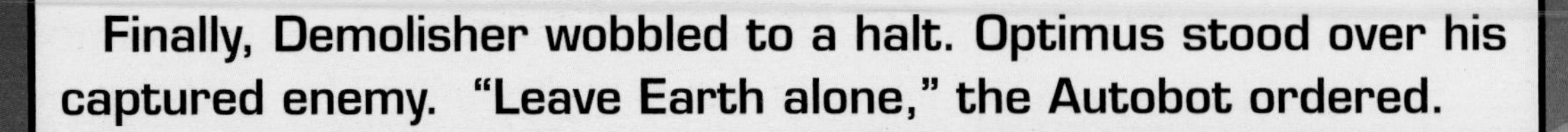

Finally, Demolisher wobbled to a halt. Optimus stood over his captured enemy. “Leave Earth alone,” the Autobot ordered.

“This is not your planet to rule . . .” Demolisher warned him, gasping for breath. “The Fallen shall rise again. . . .”

For now, the Autobots and their friends had stopped the savage Decepticons. But they knew they had to be ready. There was a bigger battle on the horizon.